Trees of Righteousness

Vicci Damiano

Trees of Righteousness
© Copyright 2011 By Vicci Damiano

ISBN 978-0-9820090-1-7

Illustrations of trees etc, unless otherwise identified, are from Dreamstime.com website

Published by
Vicci Damiano
Dove Drama Ministries
PO Box 3342
Toms River, N.J. 08756

Cover Design by Pamela Zarrello,
Ft. Lauderdale, Florida © 2011

Dedication

This Book is dedicated to my beloved husband,
Robert Francis Damiano
Aug 1, 1948 to August 6, 2004

Acknowledgments

I would especially like to recognize
James Zarrello Jr.
for his assistance in the editing of this book.

I would also like to give thanks to
Pamela Zarrello
for the beautiful Cover Design.

Likewise, I am happy to have friends like
Jim and Patty Biscardi
who have been such an inspiration and help to me
in accomplishing my goal.

Table of Contents

Preface

Trees of Righteousness

The gentle breeze blows through the tree branches
As the sweet breath of God.
The trees sway in ecstasy kissed by the Creator,
Swaying to and fro as if to say:
We glorify you, Father, for we are wonderfully made!
By Vicci © *6/20/2005*

Trees were created to bless us. Trees absorb carbon dioxide from the CO_2 molecule and release Oxygen (02) into the atmosphere giving us cleaner air. They protect the land from flooding by sponging up excess water and they add beauty to our lawns and landscapes. Meanwhile, their logs provide heat in our fireplaces and campsites. Trees also provide shade for humans and supply homes for birds and animals. Moreover, the wood from trees are used for building homes, ships, furniture, etc. Trees blossom with rainbows of flowers and seed and give fruits and nuts to eat. They also have medicinal properties and have many other uses.

Trees are inanimate objects and serve God's purposes in many different ways. At the same time, we are made after His image and likeness and are endowed with many gifts and talents. How much more should we give back to God for the beauty of our creation? How much more should we give back to God for sending His Son to die in our place? Yes, Jesus was nailed to a tree and died to make us free.

Psalm 1:1-3 *(NKJV)* states: "Blessed is the man that walks not in the counsel of the ungodly, nor stands in the way of the sinner, nor sits in the seat of the scornful, but his delight is in the law of the Lord; and in his law he meditates day and night, **and he shall be like a tree planted by the rivers of water that brings forth his fruit in due season; his leaf shall not wither nor fade and**

7

whatsoever he does shall prosper."

Holy Spirit, embrace us that we may be called **"Trees of Righteousness planted by the Lord."** *Isaiah 61:3* (NKJV) Breathe on us and use us so that Father God may be glorified in all that we do.

Introduction

"And when He was come near, even at the descent of the Mount of Olives, the whole multitude of the disciples began to rejoice and praise God with a loud voice for all the mighty works that they had seen, saying, Blessed be the King that comes in the name of the Lord: peace in heaven and glory in the highest...and some of the Pharisees from among the multitude said unto Jesus: Master, rebuke your disciples......and He answered and said unto them, **I tell you that if these should keep silent, the stones would immediately cry out.**" *Luke 19:40* (NKJV)

Psalm 150:6 (NKJV) **says: "Let everything that has breath praise the Lord,"** however, is it possible for inanimate objects to praise the Lord? The answer can be seen in I *Chronicles 16:32,33* (NKJV) **"Let the sea roar and all its fullness, let the field rejoice, and all that is in it, then the trees of the woods shall rejoice before the Lord, for He is coming to judge the earth."** In *Isaiah 55:12* (NLV) we read **"the mountains and the hills shall break forth into singing before You and all the trees of the field shall clap their hands."**

Everything that God has made was made for His honor and glory so we would have to answer, "yes," it is possible for in-animate objects to praise the Lord. The presence of all of creation, whether animate or inanimate, points to His magnificence and being.

The subject of this book is about the "Trees of the Bible." Each tree has a story to tell, and although this work does not mention all trees, it does cover but just a few important species of God's creation.

God created trees for man's use: shade, wood, fruits, etc. Trees emit oxygen and clean the air that we breathe, clean the soil, slow storm water run-off, etc. And along with these practical uses,

9

each tree of the Bible amazingly tells its own story and point to God's salvation through Jesus Christ. Why did the Savior choose death on a tree? The choice of death could have been being speared or bludgeoned to death, stoned, thrown off a cliff, etc. I believe that death on a tree (Crucifixion) had special meaning. After all, we read in the book of Genesis that the fall began with a choice. "The Tree of Life" was in the midst of the Garden of Eden as also was the "Tree of Knowledge of Good and Evil (Tree of Death)." (*Genesis* 2:9-17) The "Tree of Life" was to be a seal of eternal holiness and bliss if man had not sinned.

Read *Rev.* 22:2. Adam and Eve erred in choosing to eat from the tree of spiritual death and separation from God. They subsequently tried to cover themselves by sewing fig leaves and placing them on their bodies.(*Gen.* 3:7) But by no means was this going to cover their sin because Jesus' shed blood is the only covering for sin. Happily, Jesus Christ chose to die on a tree to give back to mankind the "Tree of Life" or a renewed relationship with God the Father. His death on the tree became our "Tree of Life." As such, He personally bore our sins in His own body on the tree and offered Himself on it, that we might die to sin and live unto the Lord, **"By whose stripes you were healed."** *I Pet.* 2:24 *(NKJV)* Thank you Jesus.

Acacia Tree or
Shittah Tree

 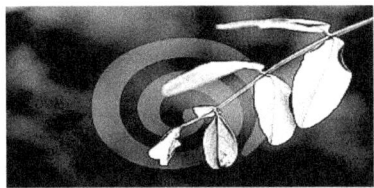

Acacia can be found growing wild in the Sinai desert and in the Jordan valley. The Hebrew word for the Acacia is the Shittah Tree. Acacia seeds are often used for food and a variety of other products. We additionally know that acacia yields gum and is used for paints and in traditional medicines for healing. Moreover, acacia is instrumental in the perfume industry due to its strong fragrance. Finally, acacia wood is durable and resistant to disease and insects, and was consequently used in shipbuilding because of its strength. (1)

In *Exodus* 25:10 & 23 God instructs Moses to use acacia wood for building the Ark of the Covenant and also the Table of Shew Bread. He was then to overlay them with gold. Symbolically, acacia tree wood represents humanity; the gold represents deity. This correspondence denotes a combination of the human and divine found in Jesus, the Son of Man and the Son of God.

Later, in *Exodus* 27, God instructs Moses to build the altar of Burnt Offering with acacia wood. In *Exodus* 30 he is also directed to build the Altar of Incense with acacia wood. At the same time, Aaron was instructed to burn sweet incense every morning when he tended to the lamps. It was in the Tabernacle that the Lord would meet with His people.

Isaiah 53:2 *(KJV)* states: "For He shall grow up before him as

(1) Sources: Heartlights Ssearch God's Word & The International Standard Bible Encyclopedia & Wikipedia, The Free Encyclopedia –Intern

a tender plant, and as a root out of a dry ground." In the New Testament, *II Peter 1:3-8* states that we have been made partakers of His divine nature. We are also roots out of dry ground and reborn to be made into golden purity. And here we have an interesting parallel: the acacia wood is resistant to disease and insects and also has healing virtues and in a similar manner Jesus was sinless and He came for us so that we can be resistant to the evils of sin and heal us. To illustrate in *I Peter 2:23, 24* (KJV) it is written of Christ, "who, when He was reviled, did not revile in return; when He suffered, He did not threaten, but committed Himself to Him who judges righteously; who Himself bore our sins in His own body on the tree, that we, having died to sins, might live for righteousness—by whose stripes you were healed."

Algum or Almug Tree aka Sandlewood

The Algum or Almug Tree is a fragrant white and yellow Sandlewood tree found in the mountains of Lebanon. (*II Chronicles 2:8-11 , I Kings 10:11*) The trees are about 9 to 12 inches through and 20 to 30 ft. high.

The algum has many uses including perfume, incense, beads, elegant boxes, cabinets, musical instruments and fans, and algum wood also polishes very nicely. Furthermore, algum was used for musical instruments such as harps and psalteries. (The psaltery, also called the nebel, was a collection of different large stringed instruments, while harps of biblical times were much smaller than today's versions.) One harp known as the kinnor was likely made of this wood. In another important function, the ingredient known as tannin – from almug wood – was mixed with sapan to make a solid, rich, red-colored dye for silks and woolen fabrics. Meanwhile, a common domestic use for sandalwood would be to act as perfume for homes with it strewn across couches. (2)

As recorded in *1 Kings 10:12* (KJV) "And the king made of the almug trees pillars for the house of the LORD, and for the king's house, harps also and psalteries for singers: there came no such almug trees, nor were seen unto this day."

And in *II Chronicles 9:10:11* (KJV) "And the servants also of Huram, and the servants of Solomon, which brought gold from

(2) Sources: David Cox's Bible Dictionary & Sandlewood Essential Oil: Victoria, Inc., & Answers.com: American Heritage Dictionary- Internet

Ophir brought algum trees and precious stones. And the king made of the algum trees terraces to the house of the Lord, and to the king's palace, and harps and psalteries for singers; and there were none such seen before in the land of Judah."

The Algum or the Sandlewood tree is symbolic of the sweet fragrance and incense used in worship. The Altar of Incense was placed in front of the veil of the Temple and on the Great Day of Atonement the High Priest could enter the Holy of Holies and raise a cloud of perfume which covered the Mercy Seat. This is symbolic of our prayers as sweet incense going up before the Lord.

We can relate the algum to the tree that Jesus died on because it symbolizes a sweet aroma of prayer, worship and song to the Father. Accordingly, Jesus is our High Priest atoning for our sins and appealing to the Father's mercy.

Almond Tree

The almond tree is the earliest to bloom during the Middle Easter Springtime, which is around February. We can relate this to Jesus being the first-fruits of the Church. The first, which is the best of the harvest, was sacred to the Lord. We may also relate this to Jesus being the first-born of all creation and the first-born from the dead. *(Col 1:14,18)* In like manner, almonds were often sent as gifts to kings and royalty. *(Gen 43:11)*

God instructed Moses to use almonds as a design on the Golden candlestick in the Holy place of the Tabernacle. *(Ex 25:33)* In this setting, there were three bowls made like unto almond with a knob and a flower in the branches coming out of the candlestick, all made of pure gold. As such, the Golden candlestick is symbolic of Christ, the light of the World and His Church, also a light. *(Rev 1:13:18)*

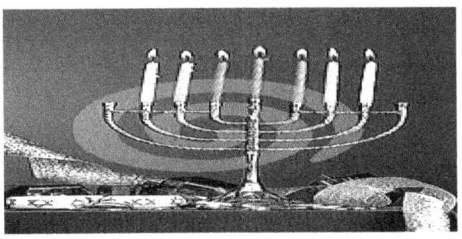

In *Numbers 16 and 17,* we read of Korah's rebellion. In Chapter 17, the Lord commanded Moses to get a rod from each of the 12 tribes of Israel with the name of the tribe written on each rod. Then Moses was to lay the rods before the Tabernacle of Witness so that the rod of the man whom the Lord chose would bud. The next day Aaron's rod budded forth into blossom and yielded ripe almonds. The Lord thus appointed Aaron of the tribe of Levi, High Priest of worship, to minister to the Lord. This budded rod was one of the 3 items contained in the Ark of the Covenant besides the 10 Commandments and the Manna.

Rods were made from a branch of a tree. They were used as a badge of authority for rulers and kings. They were also used as a shepherd's staff and as a whip; an instrument for punishment or correction. With such imagery, we can now understand more clearly the Prophecy of Jesus' coming forth in *Isaiah 11:1* (KJV) "And there shall come forth rod out of the stem of Jesse (A rod as a branch of a tree) and a Branch shall grow out of His roots; and the Spirit of the Lord shall be upon Him, the Spirit of Wisdom and Understanding, the Spirit of Counsel and Might, the Spirit of Knowledge and of the Fear of the Lord; And shall make Him of quick-understanding in the fear of the Lord and He shall not judge after the sight of His eyes neither reprove after the hearing of His ears; but with righteousness shall He judge the poor, and reprove with equity for the meek of the earth; and He shall smite the earth with the Rod of His Mouth (Word of God), and with the breath of His lips shall He slay the wicked and righteousness shall be the girdle of His loins, and faithfulness the girdle of His reins."

We can see how the blossomed rod of Aaron points to the Lord Jesus as the First-fruits, First-born, King and Ruler and High Priest. He has all authority, judges and corrects in righteousness and punishes His enemies with the Word of God as a measure of fairness. *Heb 4:12* (KJV) correspondingly says "For the Word of God is quick and powerful, and sharper than any two-edged sword, piercing even to the dividing asunder of soul and spirit and of the joints and marrow and is a discerner of the thoughts and intents of the heart." And in Hebrews *4:14* (KJV) "Seeing that we have a great High Priest, that has passed into heaven, Jesus the Son of God, let us hold fast our profession."

16

Aloe Tree aka Alahim in Hebrew

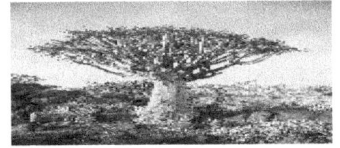 

The aloe stem bears flowers. These flowers belonging to the lily family are only two inches long and are bright vermilion and a clear, yellow. The pistil is golden yellow. (3)

Aloe was used in perfuming garments and rooms and also used as medicine. In *Psalm* 45:8 *(NKJV)* we read "Your garments are scented with myrrh and aloes and cassia." Furthermore, in *Num* 24:5-6 *(KJV)* it is written " How lovely are your tents, Oh Jacob, your dwelling places, Oh Israel like valleys they are spread out, like aloes planted by the Lord."

The aloe leaves are bluish gray and contain aloin. This substance was added to different types of incense and then dissolved in water for preparing bodies to be buried.

John 19:38 *(NKJV)* says "After this, Joseph of Arimathea, being a disciple of Jesus, but secretly for fear of the Jews, asked Pilate that he might take away the body of Jesus; and Pilate gave him permission. So he came and took the body of Jesus. And Nicodemus, who at first came to Jesus by night, also came, bringing a mixture or myrrh and **aloes,** about 100 lbs.** Then they took the body of Jesus and bound it in strips of linen with the spices, as the custom of the Jews is to bury. Now in the place where He was crucified there was a garden, and in the garden a new tomb in which no one had yet been laid. So there they laid

(3) Source: All the Plants of the Bible, Walker-Internet

17

Jesus, because of the Jews Preparation Day, for the tomb was nearby."

Christ's body was taken down from the Cross and buried on Friday, the Day of Preparation for the Sabbath. According to Jewish law, it was necessary to remove the bodies of the executed before sunset. The spices, a mixture of myrrh and **aloes,** were used to forestall decay and lessen the odor of the body.

In a metaphoric sense, Jesus is our aloe, our balm of Gilead, and our physician. He has brought recovery for the health of His people through His blood and the oil aloe of the Holy Spirit. He thusly has freed us from the stench of our rotting sin and has given us new life for eternity.

Apple Tree

The apple blossom is the flower of the Apple Tree and grows in the Spring while the apple fruit itself matures in Autumn. The apple tree was perhaps the earliest tree to be cultivated. Tapuah is a name meaning "Apple" in Hebrew. The apple tree was known in the Old Testament for its fruit, shade, beauty and fragrance. (4)

![apple fruit on tree]

Songs of Solomon Ch 2:3-4 *(NKJV)* reads "As the apple tree among the trees of the wood, so is my beloved among the sons. I sat down under his shadow with great delight, and his fruit was sweet to my taste. He brought me to the banqueting house, and his banner over me was love." Here we see a picture of the beloved's praise of her lover. Solomon was a delightful and rare find among all the other men. He was unique, sweet and fragrant as the apple tree. This Chapter also reveals three aspects of romantic love: **Protection** (sitting in his shade), **taste** (expressing knowledge of someone intimately) and **banner** (a military standard easily seen by troops as they marched; showing he was not ashamed of her). These factors enable a woman to develop a sense of security and self-worth while enjoying a stable marriage.

If we relate these factors to Jesus as the "Bridegroom"

(4) Sources: Ma Kore Hebrew & Wikipedia, the Free Encyclopedia-Internet

and the Church as the "Bride of Christ," we can determine that Jesus is a rare find and He knows each of us intimately. Who else would have loved us so much that He laid down His life to keep us from the pangs of death and to protect us from eternal damnation? He filled us with His Holy Spirit so that we may know Him intimately and develop a sense of security and self-worth in Him. He is not ashamed of us so neither should we be ashamed of His Banner, His Song and His Cross which are our military standard. In *Zechariah 2:8* and *Deut. 32:10* God describes His people as "the apple of His eye."

Bay Tree (aka Bay Laurel)

Bay Laurel Bush photo taken in Israel 2011 (Vicci)

The Bay Tree (the Hebrew word "ezrah" meaning native) is indigenous to Palestine. Bay is the same as laurel; as a wreath of bay leaves has been a classical honor given to poets and conquerors, etc. The victors in various contests, were donned with a laurel (bay) wreath signifying the honor given to one's achievements. The Bay leaf is also used in cooking and also has medicinal uses. (5)

Bay Laurel Wreath

Crown of Thorns Drawing by Vicci 2011(c)

Let us look at Our Savior and Lord, Jesus Christ. In *Matthew* 27:29 and *John* 19:2 we read that the Roman soldiers put on a crown of thorns on Jesus' head to mock Him. Thorns were a symbol of desolation (*Prov.* 24:31). His Crown of thorns was an emblem of His glory, not desolation and shame! Later, in *Revelation* 14:14, Jesus the Conquerer has a golden crown on His head! And in *Revelation* 19:12 (*KJV*) we read of Christ's triumphant return: "His eyes were as a flame of fire and on His head were many crowns." The many crowns on Christ's head represent many victories. In other words, He obtained total victory.

(5) Sources: New World Dictionary- Wikipedia, The Free Encyclopedia & Angelfire.com- Internet

The good news is that we also receive crowns, therefore, we should run the Christian race in our effort to obtain the prize, the crown of immortality. We should exert ourselves to the utmost, so that we may not fail to secure the crown of righteousness as is written in *I Cor 9:26 and I Thes 2:19*. Accordingly, in *II Tim* 4:7,8 *(NKJV)* we read Paul's words: " I have fought a good fight, I have finished the race, I have kept the faith. Finally, there is laid up for me the crown of righteousness, which the Lord, the righteous Judge, will give to me on that day; and not to me only but also to all who have loved His appearing." He wore our deserved crown of desolation and shame so that we can wear a crown of glory.

To summarize these thoughts, we read in *Revelation 4:10* *(KJV)* "The four and twenty elders fall down before him that sat on the throne, and worship him that liveth for ever and ever, and cast their crowns before the throne, saying, Thou art worthy, O Lord, to receive glory and honour and power: for thou hast created all things, and for thy pleasure they are and were created."

Cedar Tree

The cedars of Lebanon represent figuratively the glory of Israel and Christ's glory. *(Numbers 24:6 and Ezekiel 17:22)* Cedar was used in Biblical times for the building of temples, palaces and wardrobe chests because of their durable decay-resistant scented wood. Cedar wood and cedar oil is known as a natural repellent to moths and at the same time absorb moisture and deodorizes. (6)

One of the unique uses of cedar was by the temple priest in the ceremonial cleansing of lepers *(Lev 14:4,7)* The priest took two clean birds, cedar wood, scarlet and hyssop. Next, one bird was sacrificed and then cedar, scarlet and hyssop were then dipped in the blood of the dead bird. This was sprinkled upon the leper seven times and afterwards he was pronounced clean. The living bird was let loose into the open field.

This indeed gives us a picture of Jesus being killed and His blood being sprinkled on the Mercy Seat. When this sprinkling took place, we were set free just as the living bird was. We could now be declared clean of all sin, disease, and filth (we being the spiritual lepers in this case). One had to die so the other could be set free.

(6) Source: Heart lights: Search God's Word- Internet

23

Cinnamon Tree

The cinnamon tree is a genus of the evergreen and shrubs belonging to the laurel family. As such, the inner bark of several species is used to make the spice cinnamon, which is principally employed in cookery as a condiment and flavoring material. In medicine, cinnamon acts like other volatile oils and even once had a reputation as a cure for colds. It has additionally been used to treat diarrhea and other problems of the digestive system. Interestingly, cinnamon is also high in antioxidant activity. (7)

In *Songs of Solomon* 4:12-19 Solomon describes his bride as a garden with fragrant spices including cinnamon. This picture is a type of the Bride of Christ, a sweet fragrance unto the Lord.

In *Exodus* 30:22-23 Moses was instructed to use sweet smelling cinnamon in the anointing oil in the sanctuary of the Tabernacle. All the furniture in the Tabernacle was anointed with this oil and also the priests were consecrated with it. (I *Kings* 1:39 and I *Chron* 9:30) *Eccles* 7:1 states that a good name is like precious ointment and we know that Christ's name is as ointment poured forth. (*Songs of Solomon* 1:3)

In the New Testament the ingredients of the anointing oil, including cinnamon, are symbolic of the Holy Spirit whose gifts are typified by the sweet ingredients. To live the abundant life that Jesus came to give us, we need to be living and moving under the anointing of the Holy Spirit. This truth is clear from I *John* 2:20 ((NKJV) "But you have an anointing from the Holy One, and you know all things.

(7) Source: Wikipedia The Free Encyclopedia-.Internet

Cypress Tree

Cypress Trees photo taken in Israel 2011 (Vicci)

In *Genesis* 6:9-21, we read about God speaking to Noah about building an Ark. In verse 14, God specifically instructs Noah to make an Ark of Cypress wood. This is because the wood of a Cypress tree is very hard, very fine, close in grain and very durable. It has a beautiful reddish brown color and also very fragrant. (8)

With these qualities, we can see why God wanted Noah to use this wood which would be durable in water when the flood came. The Cypress has many other uses such as chests, harps, coffins, instruments, poles, planks, etc.

(8a)

We relate the Cypress tree to the Ark which was a ship of safety against an overwhelming flood of of destruction. Similarly, Jesus is our ark, our ship of safety against the flood of the world's sins and destruction. We are protected when we sail under the Flag of the Cross of Jesus Christ, and we shall land safely in His eternal kingdom.

(8) Source: Wise Geek-Internet
(8a) Noah's Ark by Edward Hicks died in 1849, copright has expired -Public Domain Art

Fig Tree

The Common Fig is a large deciduous shrub or small tree native to the Mediterranean area. There are many Scriptures which mention the Fig Tree throughout the Bible. The following are some of the Scriptures.

In *Jeremiah 24*, God showed the prophet a vision of two baskets of figs set before the temple of the Lord. One basket had very good figs and the other bad figs which could not be eaten. The Lord explained the good basket of figs as the good people who were carried away captive from Judah, but who would be kept by the Lord and given a heart to know Him. Meanwhile, the bad basket of figs were symbolic of those who remained in Egypt and whose hearts were not right towards God, therefore, they would eventually be delivered up to their enemies to be destroyed.

In the Parable of the Fig Tree in *Matthew 7:15-20* Jesus refers to men either bearing good fruit or bad fruit just like a tree; therefore, Christ said, "you will know them by their fruits."

A third example comes from *Matthew 21:18* (*NIV*): "Early in the morning, as Jesus was on his way back to the city, he was hungry. Seeing a fig tree by the road, he went up to it but found nothing on it except leaves. Then he said to it, "May you never bear fruit again!" Immediately the tree withered. When the disciples saw this, they were amazed. "How did the fig tree wither so quickly?" they asked.

The tree looked full of promise but was empty just like the city of Jerusalem and its beautiful temple. This Parable shows

God's judgment on the people of Israel who professed to follow God but produced no fruit or spiritual reality.

We can apply these parables to the Church today. Basically, they are comparing man to a fruit-bearing tree. We either bear positive fruit by having a heart towards God, obeying and doing good works or having an unrighteous heart, turning away from God and bearing the rotten fruit of sin.

Let us pray that God would give us the grace to bear good fruit for the Kingdom of God. Amen.

Fir Tree
(The Christmas Tree)

"The glory of Lebanon shall come unto you; the fir tree, the pine tree and the boxwood (cypress) together, to beautify the place of my sanctuary, and I will make the place of my feet glorious." *Isaiah 60:13 (KJV)*

The **fir, pine and boxwood trees** are all varieties of the **"evergreen."** They bloom all year round as opposed to the deciduous trees that shed their leaves and are barren until the spring time.

To decorate an evergreen tree is popular each Christmas Season in many countries, so that, The Christmas tree can have spiritual meaning for the Christian.

Most Christmas trees have a **star** or an **angel** adorning the top. This can give reference to the **"Star of Bethlehem"** which the three wise men followed looking for the new "King," the baby Jesus. **The angel** reminds us of the angels who appeared to the shepherds in the field and announced the birth of the Savior. Moreover, the **tree branches** give hint of the prophecy written in *Isaiah, 11:1 (KJV)* "And there shall come forth a rod out of the **stem of Jesse, and a Branch shall grow out of his roots** and the Spirit of the Lord shall rest upon Him." This prophesy was fulfilled with Mary, Jesus' earthly mother **coming from the line of David as did Joseph**, although he was not Jesus' natural father.

The tree is also decorated with lights, which brings to remembrance that Jesus is the " **Light of the World.**" Through His birth, he offers us life, light, wisdom and hope for a dying world. Furthermore, because the evergreen blooms all year round it can represent the **"eternal life"** which Jesus give us through His death and resurrection. The decorations, meanwhile, become a part of the tree and are added on for more beauty. They are a reminder of **the body of Christ with all of its gifts** working in harmony to beautify the Kingdom of God.

In many places it is not politically correct to display a creche or nativity scene, however, every time we see a Christmas tree, it can tell the story of Jesus' birth. The glory of Lebanon, who is Jesus the Messiah, has come unto us as a **"Tree of Life"** bringing salvation. We as the temple of the Holy Ghost are His sanctuary, the place where He resides and rests..

"Arise, shine, for thy light is come and the glory of the Lord is risen upon you." *Isaiah 60:1* *(KJV)*

Juniper Tree
aka The Broom Tree

The Juniper tree is called the Broom tree in the Bible and is more of a large shrub than a tree reaching heights up to 12 feet. (9)

We can read in *I Kings 19:4* that when the prophet Elijah fled to the desert to hide from Jezebel who wanted to kill him, he lay down under the Broom tree (juniperus) for protection. There he was sheltered from the sun during the day and from the wind at night. Then an angel of the Lord came to Elijah to minister food and drink to him for his journey as he rested under the tree.

We also hide under the Tree (the Cross) of Jesus. He died on the tree to save us from our enemy, the accuser of the brethern: "Therefore, there is now no condemnation to those who are in Christ Jesus because through Christ Jesus the law of the Spirit who gives life has set you free from the law of sin and and death." *Romans 8:1 (NIV)* He also feeds us as we travel through the wilderness in this world for He is the bread of Life and we drink of His cup of salvation which leads to eternal life.

(9) Source: Juniper in the Bible-From *Plants of the Bible*, H.N. & A.L. Moldenke -Internet

Locust Tree
aka Carob Tree

The Carob tree is a Locust variety (evergreen species) and is of the pea family. It is cultivated for its pea pods. (10)

Matthew 3:4 *(NKJV)* states "Now John (St. John the Baptist) himself was clothed in camel's hair with a leather belt around his waist; and his food was locusts and wild honey." Carobs are also know as St. John's bread because some Christians think that this is what he ate in the desert. This belief seems to come from a transcriber substituting the Hebrew "G" for the "R" in cherev which turns the word from carob to locust. However, there is no proof of whether he actually ate grasshoppers or fruit from the locust tree (Carob variety).

Dried carob fruit is traditionally eaten on the Jewish holiday of Tu Bishvat. This is a minor Jewish holiday usually sometime in late January or early February that marks the "New Year of the Trees." The holiday has to do with the blessings of God's provision of fruit from the trees and also with tithing. (10)

With this background in mind, we can see that the Locust Tree (Carob variety) speaks to us of God's blessings and provisions.

(10) Source: Wikopedia, The Free Encyclopedia

Mulberry Tree

Mulberry TreePhoto taken in Israel 2011 (Vicci)

Worldwide, the Mulberry Tree is grown for its fruit. In traditional and folk medicine, the fruit is believed to have medicinal properties and is used for making jam, wine, and other food products. (11)

In *I Chronicles 14:13* and *II Samuel 5:22*-25 we read about David fighting the Philistines in the Valley of Raphaim. David inquired of the Lord and was instructed by Him to take his army of men in front of the mulberry trees. "And the Philistines yet again spread themselves abroad in the valley. Therefore David inquired again of God; and God said unto him, Go not up after them; turn away from them, and come upon them over against the mulberry trees. And it shall be, when thou shalt hear a sound of going in the tops of the mulberry trees, that then thou shalt go out to battle: for God is gone forth before thee to smite the host of the Philistines. David therefore did as God commanded him: and they smote the host of the Philistines from Gibeon even to Gazer."

The Lord fought the battle for David against the evil Philistines with His own army of angels marching atop of the mulberry trees. Again, The Lord Jesus fought the battle of sin and evil for us and he used the tree at Calvary.

(11) Source: Dave's Garden - Internet

Mustard Seed Tree

Mustard seeds are typically about 1 or 2mm in diameter, may be colored from yellowish white to black, and they are used as spices in many regional cuisines. Moreover, the mustard seed produces oil for cooking and is a source of protein. Although it is more of a shrub than a tree it can grow to 10 ft tall. Thus, it can become a large sanctuary for the birds of the air. (12)

Jesus tells the parable of the mustard seed in *Matthew 13:31-32 (NIV)* "The kingdom of heaven is like a mustard seed, which a man took and planted in his field. Though it is the smallest of all your seeds, yet when it grows, it is the largest of garden plants and becomes a tree, so that the birds of the air come and perch in its branches."

In this metaphor, Jesus is the planter who came to atone for our sins to make us fruitful. Meanwhile, the Tree is rooted in Jesus and has grown far beyond what was planted offering a refuge for all those who come to Him. At the same time, the field represents the people who will receive Him while the mustard seed is the Gospel which starts out small and then is spread throughout the whole world. Overall, the tiny mustard seed that grows to be a large tree, symbolizes Jesus' offer of refuge and life in God's Kingdom.

(12) Source: Wikipedia The Free Encylopedia and CARM websites

Oak Tree (aka as Terebinth or Quercus Tree)

 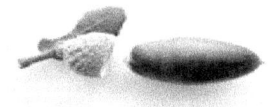

The Oak is a common symbol of strength and endurance and has been chosen as the national tree of many countries. The flowers are catkins produced in the spring and the fruit is a nut called an acorn born in a cup-like structure known as a cupule. Due to its durability, oak is used in the construction of buildings, ships, etc. Today oak wood is also commonly used for furniture and flooring, timber frame buildings and additionally for veneer production. (13)

In *Joshua* 24:25-28 we read that Joshua made a covenant with the Lord; the Israelites were to serve The Lord God and not to serve any foreign gods. Joshua wrote this statute and ordinance in the Book of the Law of God. He took a large stone and set it up under an oak tree at Shechem by the Sanctuary of the Lord. Shechem means "shoulder or strength." The stone under the oak tree functioned as a legal reminder or a covenant that the people entered into where they repented from their sins, errors and idol worship. They now wanted to serve the Lord and to thank Him for the victories they had won. Previously in *Genesis* 35:4 Jacob had made a covenant that the Israelites would serve the Lord. He collected all the false idols that the people were worshiping and buried them beneath the oak tree at Shechem. This is believed to be the same tree.

Let us compare this with the Covenant that Jesus has made with us when He was crucified on the Tree. Because of Jesus' strength and endurance in dying for our sins, the old was done away with and the New Covenant came into existence. As long as we enter into covenant with Him, get rid of all false idols, repent of our sin and follow Him alone, we are given new and eternal life

(13) Source: Wikipedia The Free Encyclopedia-Internet

and blessings. The legal reminder of Our New Covenant is the Tree He died on and the Stone that was rolled back from His grave when He rose from the dead.

Olive Tree

Olive Tree Photo taken in Garden of Gethsemane, Israel 2011 (Vicci) Olive Leaf Photo Israel 2011

The Olive   is an evergreen tree or shrub native to the Mediterranean, Asia and Africa. The olive tree has many uses as we know: olives, olive oil, olive wood, etc. Also, the natural olive leaf and olive leaf extracts are used as anti-aging agents for the immune system and as antibiotics. As such, clinical evidence has proven the blood pressure lowering effects of the carefully extracted olive leaf. (14)

Drawing of Olive Wreath and Peace Dove by Vicci

The Olive Tree has been very symbolic throughout the Bible. For example, the leafy branches of the olive tree have been used as a symbol of **abundance, glory and peace**. The leaves were used to crown the victors of friendly games and also war conquerors as emblems of **benediction and purification.** For the Christian, Jesus is our abundance, glory and peace. He has blessed and purified us through His blood which was shed on the Cross.

It was an Olive leaf that the Dove brought back to Noah to demonstrate that the flood was over. (*Gen* 8:11) In this case, it was clearly a symbol of peace.

The olive tree was also an important factor when Solomon built the Temple. "For the entrance of the inner sanctuary he made doors of olive wood; the lintel and doorposts were one-fifth of the wall. The two doors were of olive wood; and he carved on them figures of cherubim, palm trees and open flowers and overlaid them with gold; he spread gold on the cherubim and on the palm trees. So for the door of the sanctuary he also made doorposts of

(14) Source: Wikipedia, The Free Encyclopedia and Web MD-Internet

43

olive wood, one-fourth of the olive wood, one-fourth of the wall."
I *Kings* 6:31-33 (NKJV) Again, the olive here is a **symbol of abundance, glory and peace.**

In *Jeremiah* 11:16 (NKJV) "The Lord called your name, **Green Olive Tree, Lovely and Good Fruit**: with the noise of a great tumult he has kindled fire on it, and its branches are broken." Jeremiah is speaking of the Israelites as a green olive tree chosen by the Lord. It speaks of judgment when the people sin against God. This can also be prophetic for the future of those Jews who did not believe in Jesus as Messiah when He came. In Psalms 52:8 (KJV) David speaks of **beauty and righteousness:** "But I am like a green olive tree in the house of God: I trust in the mercy of God forever and ever. I will praise you forever." Verse 52: 6 states that the righteous shall see and fear.

In the New Testament in *Romans* 11:17 (NIV) we read, "If some of the branches have been broken off, and you, though a wild olive shoot, have been grafted in among the others and now share in the nourishing sap from the olive root, do not consider yourself to be superior to those other branches. If you do, consider this: You do not support the root, but the root supports you. You will say then, "Branches were broken off so that I could be grafted in. Granted. But they were broken off because of unbelief, and you stand by faith. Do not be arrogant, but tremble. For if God did not spare the natural branches, he will not spare you either." Paul is speaking here of the gentiles being grafted into the Abrahamic Covenant and having become recipients of God's blessing. From this illustration, we learn that the gentile believers should not boast about their acceptance from God nor despise the Jews.

Later, *Revelation* 11:3-4 (KJV) speaks of the two witnesses as olive trees "And I will give power unto my two witnesses, and they shall prophesy a thousand two hundred and threescore days, clothed in sackcloth. These are the two olive trees, and the two candlesticks standing before the God of the earth." **The olive tree represents the source of oil and the lamp stand represents the church converting the olive oil and light is received.. This light** guides the footsteps of the members. Therefore, consider that **the** olive trees represent the Word of God (which enlighten men) and the Light Stand represents the Church who is to witness the light of the gospel to others. Also of interest, the two witnesses refers to the Old Testament Witness and the New Testament Witness. As an example the writings of Moses, Daniel, Paul and others form the Olive tree witness. Through such men olive oil is received by the church. In addition, the sackcloth clothing of the two witnesses portrays the nature of their witness. Their role was to provide the testimony of God. They were to exercise humility, while delivering the message with an appropriate level of certainty. We can summarize by stating that the **Two Olive Trees represent: The Law and the Prophets while the lamp stand represents the Old Covenant Church and the New Testament Church.** (15)

The Garden of Gethsemane is located on a slope of the Mount of Olives near Jerusalem and where Jesus prayed on the night He was betrayed. **Gethsemane means "oil press"** and figuratively speaks of **anointing and fruitfulness."** A garden of ancient olive trees stands there to this day. Jesus frequently went to Gethsemane with His disciples to pray *(John 18)*. On the night of His betrayal, Jesus was under severe pressure in the Garden of Gethsemane, while he struggled in prayer - releasing his burden to the Father's will "if it be possible, let this cup pass from me: nevertheless not as I will, but as thou wilt." *Matthew 26:39* (KJV)

As the fruit of the olive tree is pressed and crushed to obtain pure olive oil, Jesus was pressed and crushed to obtain salvation for us that we may be purified before the Father. **He has given us the oil of joy for mourning and the garment of praise for the spirit of heaviness. *Isaiah 61:3***

Photo of Olive Press taken in Israel 2011 (Vicci)

(15) Source: Information based on Bible insight.com

45

Palm Tree

Palm Tree Photos taken in Israel 2011 (Vicci)

Palms have large evergreen leaves that are either fan-leaved or feather-leaved compound and spirally arranged at the top of the stem. There are many varieties of palm trees. More than two thirds of palm species live in tropical areas. Forest Palms may also live in grasslands and scrub lands, usually associated with a water source, and in desert oases such as the Date Palm.

The Date Palm provides a concentrated energy food which could be easily stored and carried along on long journey across the deserts. The tree also creates a habitat for people to live in by providing shade and protection from the desert winds.

The palm branch was a **symbol of triumph and victory**. The Romans rewarded champions of the games and celebrated military successes with palm branches. (16)

The Palm also **represents peace and plenty** and is one of the Four Species of **Sukkot** aka **the Feast of Booths or The Feast of Tabernacles**. The **Lulav** (Palm leaf) is used in the morning prayer services during the Feast of Booths. The other species of leaves used are myrtle, willow and citron which are wrapped around the palm. We can read about this in *Leviticus 23:39-43*. The user brings his or her hands together and waves the species in all four directions (plus up and down) to attest to God's mastery over all of creation. This ritual also symbolically voices a prayer

(16) Sources: 20/20 Site -Internet

47

for adequate rainfall over all the earth's vegetation in the coming year. This **waving ceremony** was performed in the Holy Temple for seven Days and elsewhere only on the first day. The feast of **Sukkot** is also detailed in the Book of *Nehemiah 8:13-18*. It was a **celebration of harvest and thanksgiving for God's protection** of His people, preserving them when they lived in the wilderness. The booths which were made of olive branches, oil trees, myrtle branches, palm branches and leafy tree leaves, symbolizes how the Lord brought Israel out of Egypt and they lived in booths. (17)

We read of the **"Triumphal Entry"** of Jesus into Jerusalem which we presently call Palm Sunday in *John 12:15* (*NIV*) "The next day the great crowd that had come for the festival heard that Jesus was on his way to Jerusalem. They took palm branches and went out to meet him, shouting, "Hosanna!" "Blessed is he who comes in the name of the Lord!" "Blessed is the king of Israel!" Jesus found a young donkey and sat on it, as it is written: "Do not be afraid, Daughter Zion; see, your king is coming, seated on a donkey's colt."

In *Zechariah 9:9* *(KJV)* we can read of this prophecy "Rejoice greatly, O daughter of Zion; shout, O daughter of Jerusalem: behold, thy King cometh unto thee: he is just, and having salvation; lowly, and riding upon an ass, and upon a colt the foal of an ass."

When the people waved the palm leaves it had such meaning. First, it was symbolic of Jesus as the **Triumphant King**. Waving of the Palms was also symbolic of a **New Covenant Provision** for His people. It shows prophetically that through "His Wave Offering" (our King's love, death and Resurrection), His people were redeemed so that they could have new life and obtain

(17) Judaism 101- Internet

an abundance of peace, blessings and prosperity sealed with His protection. The **Symbolic Feast of Booths** shows that He also took us out of the wandering wilderness into a New Life and relationship with our God. He covers us with His Blood of Redemption and fills us with the Holy Spirit, our Palm leaf of protection.

Rev 7:9 *(KJV)* "After this I beheld, and, lo, a great multitude, which no man could number, of all nations, and kindreds, and people, and tongues, stood before the throne, and before the Lamb, clothed with white robes, a**nd palms in their hands**; And cried with a loud voice, saying, Salvation to our God which sitteth upon the throne, and unto the Lamb. And all the angels stood round about the throne, and about the elders and the four beasts, and fell before the throne on their faces, and worshiped God, Saying, Amen: Blessing, and glory, and wisdom, and thanksgiving, and honor, and power, and might, be unto our God for ever and ever. Amen."

We shall also be with Jesus in great happiness and joy praising Him forever and ever giving Him a great Wave offering to thank Him for His triumph over sin and death and for setting us free. We can lift the palm of our hands to worship Him now and for eternity.

Pomegranate Tree

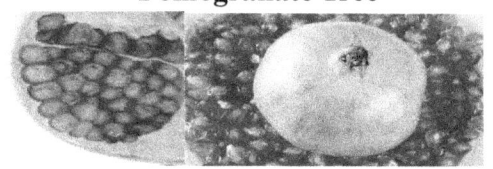

The Pomegranate tree is native to ancient Persia and was cultivated over the whole Mediterranean region since the beginning of written history. Its popularity is primarily driven by the proven fact of its strong anti-oxidant properties. It has many medicinal qualities. The Hebrew word for "pomegranate" is *Ramam*, which means "to rise up" or "to be mounted up" (18) "But they that wait upon the LORD shall renew their strength; they shall **mount up** with wings as eagles; they shall run, and not be weary; and they shall walk, and not faint." *Isaiah 40:31 (KJV)*

The pomegranate was one of the fruits that Joshua and the others brought back when they went out to spy the land of Canaan. These fruits showed how fertile the land was. Carved figures of the pomegranate were principal ornaments adorning stately columns and pillars in Solomon's temple.

When the High Priest ministered in the temple, he wore special garments. At the bottom of the high priest's robe were pomegranates and gold bells. The gold bells were symbolic of purity ringing out to declare salvation and life. The intertwined red, blue and purple pomegranates were also symbols of life and abundance. (*Exodus 28:33*)

Solomon describes his bride: "your temples behind your veil are like a piece of pomegranate." *Song of Solomon 4:3 (NIV)* This is symbolic of sweetness, life and abundance. Notice the symbolism, "Temple behind the Veil" would be the Holy Place

(18)Sources: Wikipedia, The Free Encyclopedia & The Priestly Garments – Internet

for the veil separated the Holy of Holies from the rest of the temple building. Therefore, we are talking about fellowship with the Lord. We are talking about the Bride (the Church) having the mind of Christ and being in the presence of her Lord and Savior.

We can summarize through these Bible verses that the pomegranate shows a picture of life, abundance and fruitfulness which characters the Savior's bride, The Church. Our Father, let thy Kingdom of life, abundance and fruitfulness come on earth as it is in heaven.

Sycamore Tree aka Sycamine

The Sycamore or Scyamine Tree belongs to the same family as the fig tree. Its name comes from the Greek "sicon" fig and "moros" blackberry bush. The Sycamore has leaves similar to the blackberry bush and fruit similar to the fig. However, it is considered insipid or not as tasty as the regular mulberry tree. The fruit of the Sycamore was considered as humble food. It grows naturally in Lebanon, Arabia, Israel and Egypt. (19)

In *Amos 7:14* we see that Amos said that he was a sheepherder and a gatherer of scycamore fruit. He expressed the fact that he belongs to a humble class of the community by calling himself a gatherer of sycamore fruit God took him and made him prophet to herd men, not sheep, so they he could bear fruit for the God's Kingdom.

We are familiar with Zacchaeus *(Luke 19:4)* when he was short of stature and was so passionate to see Jesus that he climbed the Sycamore tree. Zacchaeus went up into the Sycamore because it was large, able to bear him and he could have a full view of Christ. Jesus said, "Zacchaeus, make haste and come down, for today I must abide at your house." *Luke 19:5 (KJV)* So Zacchaeus quickly came down and received Him joyfully. Zaccheus is declared to be a happy man because he turned from sin to God and was not ashamed to do this publicly.

(19) Sources:20/20 Site

Rev 3:20 (NKJV) says "Behold I stand at the door and knock; if anyone hears My voice and opens the door, I will come in to him and dine with him and he with Me. To him, who overcomes, I will grant to sit with Me on my throne, as I also overcame and sat down with My Father on His throne. He who has an ear, let him hear what the Spirit says to the churches."

The Lord knocked at the door of the hearts of both Amos and Zacchaeus; The Sycamore Tree lending meaning to the humility of both of these mens' hearts. They both accepted the Lord's calling, supped with the Lord and bore fruit by gathering men to the truth of the Lord.

Willow Tree

Willows all have an abundant watery bark which is charged with salicyoic acid which have been used in ancient times for aches and fever. Willow wood is used to manufacture various furniture, toys and other articles; its fiber is used for baskets, rope, etc. The Willow tree is ecologically useful for land use and water stabilization, etc. It is popular to call the tree "Weeping Willow" because it droops down and is related with human weeping. (20)

In Psalm 137 (NKJV) the Psalmist writes "By the rivers of Babylon,There we sat down, yea, we wept when we remembered Zion. We hung our harps upon the willows in the midst of it. for there those who carried us away captive asked of us a song, And those who plundered us requested mirth, saying, "Sing us *one* of the songs of Zion!" How shall we sing the Lord's song in a foreign land? If I forget you, O Jerusalem, Let my right hand forget its skill*!"*

The Jews were taken captive in Babylon and they related their suffering in this Psalm. It is ironic that they related their weeping to the Willow tree. They rejoiced after 70 years when they were free to return to Jerusalem and re-build the Temple.

We also weep about the Tree that Jesus was crucified on but we also rejoice that because of His Death and Resurrection we have a new life of freedom in Him. He built His temple in us.

(20) Sources: Wikipedia, The Free Encyclopedia & The Weeping Willow by swift - Internet

What joy! We are the temple of the Holy Spirit! It is written in *Psalms* 30:5 (*NKJV*) "Weeping endures for the night but joy comes in the Morning (new dawn) or the *NIV* version: "For his anger lasts only a moment, but his favor lasts a lifetime; weeping may stay for the night, but rejoicing comes in the morning."

Conclusion

I hope that this book has given you insight into how humans, trees and all creation have been made for God's purpose and how all should glorify the Creator. If you never realized why you were created and would like to fulfill your purpose, there are certain principals written in the Word of God that show you what you can do. This is why it is important to read the Bible.

When Adam and Eve sinned by disobedience and ate of the Tree of Good and Evil all mankind was doomed to a sinful nature, death and separation from God. "But you must not eat from the Tree of the Knowledge of Good and Evil, for when you eat of it you will surely die" *Gen 2:17* (*NIV*) God the Father sent His Son Jesus to die on the Cross so that through His loving sacrifice mankind would be redeemed and be re-united with Him. "For God so loved the world that he gave his one and only Son, that whoever believes in him shall not perish but have eternal life." *John 3:16* (*NIV*) His Cross is our Tree of Life.

Jesus said, "Truly, truly, I say to you, unless one is born of water (Word of God) and the Spirit, he cannot enter into the Kingdom of God." John 3:5 (*NAS*) Jesus sent His Holy Spirit to live within the believers' spirits so as to love, guide, comfort, teach and give new life. The Lord desires a close relationship with us. "Jesus answered and said to him, "If anyone loves Me, he will keep My word; and My Father will love him, and We will come to him and make Our home with him. *John 14:23* (*NKJV*)

Once we accept these truths and ask God's forgiveness for our sins in not obeying His Word, we can live a new life and be filled with His Holy Spirit. "Repent and believe in the gospel." *Mark 1:15* (*NKJV*) Also, when our life is finished on this earth, we will live a glorious life with Him for eternity.

We should seek Him daily through prayer to grow into a close relationship with Him for this is what He desires; our fellowship.

One cannot be intimate with Him unless the relationship is nurtured. "Here I am! I stand at the door and knock. If anyone hears my voice and opens the door, I will come in and eat with that person, and they with me." *Rev 3:20* (NIV)

If you earnestly and truthfully desire the new life that the Lord has provided for us and **Accept, Admit, Repent and Ask**, you will be on your way to a glorious path.

1. **Accept:** Jesus' loving sacrifice and redemption of the Cross.
2. **Admit:** We are disobedient sinners as Adam and Eve were.
3. **Repent:** Ask Jesus to forgive our sins and cleanse us so that He can give us His Holy Spirit in order that we may live a righteous life and obey His commands.
4. **Seek:** Him daily through prayer and the Word to grow in Him.

May the Lord bless you with new life and guide you so that you will be a Tree of Righteousness and bear much fruit for His Kingdom.. Amen.

Psalm 148 (KJV) Praise ye the Lord. Praise ye the Lord from the heavens: praise him in the heights. Praise ye him, all his angels: praise ye him, all his hosts. Praise ye him, sun and moon: praise him, all ye stars of light. Praise him, ye heavens of heavens, and ye waters that be above the heavens. Let them praise the name of the LORD: for he commanded, and they were created. He hath also stablished them for ever and ever: he hath made a decree which shall not pass. Praise the LORD from the earth, ye dragons, and all deeps: Fire, and hail; snow, and vapours; stormy wind fulfilling his word: Mountains, and all hills; **fruitful trees, and all cedars:** Beasts, and all cattle; creeping things, and flying fowl: Kings of the earth, and all people; princes, and all judges of the earth: Both young men, and maidens; old men, and children: Let them praise the name of the LORD: for his name alone is excellent; his glory is above the earth and heaven. He also exalteth the horn (strength) of his people, the praise of all his saints; even of the children of Israel, a people near unto him. Praise ye the Lord.